WAR
IS
OVER

WAR
IS
OVER

David Almond

illustrated by
David Litchfield

CANDLEWICK PRESS

Text copyright © 2018 by David Almond
Illustrations copyright © 2018 by David Litchfield

First U.S. edition 2020
First published by Hachette Children's Group (U.K.) 2018

Library of Congress Catalog Card Number pending
ISBN 978-1-5362-0986-0

20 21 22 23 24 25 LBM 10 9 8 7 6 5 4 3 2 1

Printed in Melrose Park, IL, U.S.A.

This book was typeset in Minion Pro.
The illustrations were done in pen, ink, and watercolor.

Candlewick Press
99 Dover Street
Somerville, Massachusetts 02144

visit us at www.candlewick.com

A JUNIOR LIBRARY GUILD SELECTION

For Anne McNeil

John first saw Jan, the German boy, on the day of the visit to the munitions factory.

It was just along the river from John's home.

It was just down the street from where he went to school.

All the years that he'd been growing up, it had been getting bigger, bigger, and when the war started it got even bigger and kept on getting bigger. It was over a mile long now. John could hardly remember what it was like before, just like he could hardly remember what *he* was like before, in those distant days before the war.

It was the biggest munitions factory in the world. Warships were built there. Guns and bombs and shells were made there. It was where John's mother worked, where so many of the mothers worked. They did twelve-hour shifts. They did overtime, double time. They worked harder, harder, longer, longer.

At shift's start and shift's end, the streets were filled with streams of blue-uniformed women making their way from their houses to the factory gates and back again.

The streets would be filled

with their footsteps,

their chatter,

their laughter,

their songs.

Beneath the vibrant sounds of these women, there was the constant clatter of the machines and engines making the instruments of war. And once in a while there'd be the noise of an explosion when time seemed to stop and all the children held their breath and whispered, "Please, God, not my mam, not this time."

That was where Mr. McTavish, the head teacher, would take the children that day, to see how great their nation was, to see that victory would soon be theirs.

"This place is where your mothers work," he told them, "to make the weapons that will keep your fathers safe."

Before they all set off, he inspected necks and ears.

He slapped Joseph Waggott on the cheek.

He thumped Oliver Tomes in the chest.

"Filthy beasts," he snarled. "Such filth might be good enough for German boys. Don't you know that cleanliness is next to godliness?"

He stood erect before the children in his jet-black suit, then led them in the national anthem and in a prayer for peace. He held his fist to his chest, then thrust it high into the air.

"Any sign of stupidity . . ." he said.

He thumped the air in warning, and off they went.

John's mam had never wanted to tell him what she did in there, except to say that she worked in somewhere called the shell shop. But when Mr. McTavish announced the visit, John asked her again to tell him more. She used a pencil and some paper. She drew the shape of a shell standing up straight. She drew so well. It had beautiful curves. At the top it was flat where he'd imagined it would be pointed. There was an opening there.

"That's where I pour the shrapnel in," she said.

"The shrapnel?"

"Lots of little lead balls. I mix them with liquid resin, then I pour it all in. Then I screw the top of the shell on. The resin sets inside and keeps the lead in place."

She drew the shell as if it was opened up, with the lead balls packed tight inside it.

She shrugged.

"Then the shells are taken away on a ship or a train and carried down to France."

She turned away and cut a slice of bread. She spread butter and jam on it and passed it down to her son. He took it and started to eat.

"What does the shrapnel do?" he asked.

She reached out and touched his cheek.

"When the shell gets close to its target, it explodes and all the shrapnel scatters out."

"And kills the Germans?"

"Yes. And kills the Germans."

The boy saw the shell exploding in his mind.

He looked at the picture of his dad and mam and himself on the wall, the one he'd drawn when he was four years old. It showed them walking together in the woods beyond the town before the war. Birds flew in the bright-blue air and a huge yellow sun shone.

"Do the Germans have shrapnel shells as well?" he asked.

"Everyone has shrapnel shells."

"But we have more?"

"Yes, John. We're told that we have many more."

"And Dad has a steel helmet?"

"Yes. We make them in the factory, too."

"When will the war be over, Mam?"

"Oh, love. They say it can't be long, not now."

He ate his bread and jam.

It was rose-hip jam. She'd made it last autumn, from the hips they'd gathered together one Sunday afternoon. As he ate, she turned over the picture of the shrapnel shell. She drew a picture of a rose hip on the other side. She drew the hip as if it had been sliced open, to show all the tiny seeds packed tight in there, all those little seeds of life.

When will the war be over? It was what John kept asking, what everyone kept asking. Would it all go on forever? Would the munitions factory keep growing and growing forever? Would it never come to an end?

He told nobody about it, but he'd written a letter to the king. He put it into an envelope addressed to Buckingham Palace and put it into the postbox on Kitchener Street. They'd learned at school about how to address a king, but they were never expected to actually do it.

"Please, Your Majesty," he wrote. "Can you tell me when it will be over?"

There was no answer.

He wrote to the Archbishop of Canterbury in Lambeth Palace, for they'd learned about archbishops, too.

"Please, Your Grace. I'm scared. My dad is in the trenches and my mam is in the shell shop and I need to know when it will be over."

There was no answer.

At school there were no answers.

"We are all at war," said Mr. McTavish. "We are all engaged in the fight to defeat the evil German."

Someone dared to raise a hand and ask, "Sir, we are children. How can we fight? How can we be at war?"

It was Dorothy Simpson, a girl from Craster Row.

He glared all the harder.

"You fight by being good children," he said. "By getting on with your work, by doing your chores, by saying your prayers."

"But, sir . . ." continued Dorothy.

"Ask no more!" snapped McTavish. "Be good. Do your work. Say your prayers!"

He lashed his cane down onto his desk.

He pointed at her.

"We know about people like you," he said.

She asked no more. None of the children asked more.

Even when fathers died, such as the father of Colin Atkinson or the father of Cicely Grey, or when the mother of Thomas Charlton lost her leg in the factory, none of the children asked more.

They tried to be good children. John tried to be a good boy. He knelt by the bed and said his prayers each night.

"I know that you are on our side, Lord. Please heed my prayer. Please protect my mam and dad. Please bring it to an end."

But each morning he woke and there seemed to be no end to come. The war continued. The munitions factory grew and grew.

And in the secret chambers of his heart, he kept on daring to ask himself, *I am just a child. How can I be at war?*

The sun shone brightly and the air was cold as they filed out through the steel school gates.

"Left, right, left, right!" called Mr. McTavish. "One, two, one, two!"

They walked in pairs. Alec Bly was at John's side.

Some of the girls turned the marching step into a dance. They turned the teacher's words into the lines of a song, a dancing song, a skipping song. They laughed again, more secretly, when McTavish stopped and turned and held his hand against the sun and warned

them, "There will be trouble to pay for those who act the fool today."

"I could lob a half brick," Alec said as they marched on, "hit him dead on the head and bring him down."

He feigned doing this.

"Kapow!" he said. **"Kaboom!"**

John grinned at the bloodied image they shared.

"Been practicing," said Alec. "I hit two rabbits, a pigeon and a daft old dog last Sunday afternoon."

He contemplated the imaginary grenade that rested in his fist.

The din of the munitions factory intensified.

They passed the post office and the co-op, where a neighbor, Mrs. McNulty, held a loaf of

bread in her hand and saluted. Outside Hall's
Newsagents a billboard asked:

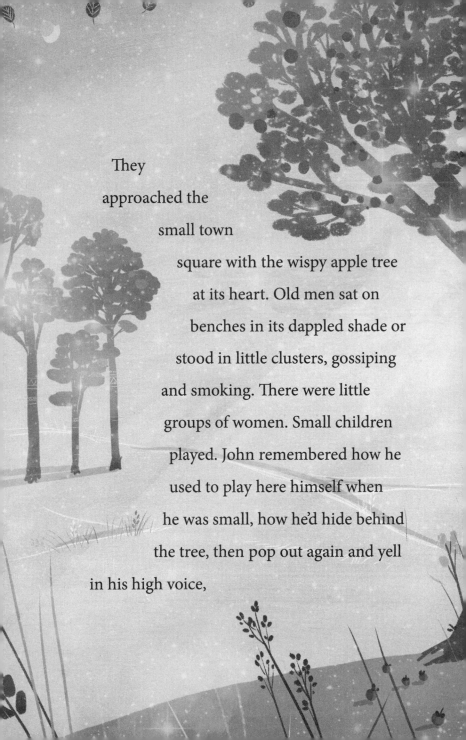

They
approached the
small town
square with the wispy apple tree
at its heart. Old men sat on
benches in its dappled shade or
stood in little clusters, gossiping
and smoking. There were little
groups of women. Small children
played. John remembered how he
used to play here himself when
he was small, how he'd hide behind
the tree, then pop out again and yell
in his high voice,

"Here
I am,
Mammy!"

The factory loomed
closer.
It towered over
the terraced houses
that led toward it.

Its

dark

shadow

fell

across

the

streets.

John turned his eyes to the woods and hills at the far edge of town. It was the place where children liked to play. It was the place where John's mam said they would walk as a family when Dad was home again. John tried to imagine that and tried to imagine the sunlight and birdsong that would surround them, tried to imagine his mam singing her favorite songs. Then he panicked as he marched one-two, one-two. He suddenly knew that he could hardly remember what his father looked like. He tried in vain to bring the beloved face and voice back to his mind.

Alec punched John in the ribs and brought him out of it.

"Look at this!" he said.

A white-haired man had appeared at the center of the square, close by the apple tree. He stood on a box with his hands raised to the sky. He was yelling something that John could not hear. He was waving papers that John could not see.

McTavish spread his own arms out straight, a barrier that brought the children to a halt.

"Suffer little children!"

yelled the man on the box.

"Let them come forward!"

Men came to the door of the Hanged Man pub at the edge of the square.

"Clear off, coward!" someone yelled.

"Shove off, ye damn traitor!"

Three men edged toward him. One of them cast his jacket off and rolled his shirtsleeves up.

"Poor soul," said Dorothy, coming to John's side.

"Coward!" yelled Alec. "Conchie scum!"

"It's my Uncle Gordon," said Dorothy.

John looked. He'd heard about this man, about other men like him. They were loudly cursed, or spoken about in whispers.

"My family have nowt to do with him any more," said Dorothy. "After the last time, we thought he'd gone into hiding in the woods."

"The last time?" said John.

"Aye. It looked like they might kill him."

"Looks like he's gone wild," said Alec. "Looks like a blasted madman."

Uncle Gordon saw the men coming for him. He saw the group of women coming for him, too. He jumped from his box and ran to the children. McTavish tried to stand in his way, but Gordon elbowed him aside and came to the children. They'd broken from their pairs. Some of them cringed in fear, some of them stood up to him with fists clenched, some giggled, some curled their lips and sneered.

"You are not at war, children!" he yelled. "You are children! Do not believe them when they say you are at war!"

McTavish put a hand on his shoulder, but Gordon shrugged him away.

He waved his papers.

"Look," he told them. "These are children just like you."

There were faces on the papers. Drawings, blurred etchings.

"Are they monsters?" asked Gordon. "Are they demons? No, they are children just like you."

The three men were at him now, thumping him, dragging him away.

"They are German children, children. I have been there. I have seen them. They are children, just like you. They have fathers, they have brothers, they have sisters, they have mothers just like you."

Then he was down on the ground and the papers were scattered and the men were punching and kicking and McTavish was guiding the children away.

"There are no monsters!" yelled Gordon in a strangled voice. "There are only lies! There is no need for war!"

McTavish commanded the children to turn away.

"The man is a well-known coward," he said.

"He has refused to fight. He is a well-known traitor and blasphemer. He should not be among us."

The children heard Gordon's cries of pain.

They could no longer be made not to look.

And here came two policemen, running, and Gordon's attackers backed away toward the doors of the Hanged Man.

The policemen hauled Gordon to his feet. There was blood on his face and tears fell from his eyes.

The policemen checked his wounds. They snarled their warnings.

"He's been told before," said Dorothy. "He was told to never come back again. Maybe this time they'll throw him into jail."

Two women crossed the square and came to Gordon and the policemen.

"He went to Germany before the war," continued Dorothy. "He said it was lovely."

The women held out two white feathers to the white-haired man.

"He's had those before as well," said Dorothy.

The policemen shoved the feathers into Gordon's collar and dragged him away, past the wizened apple tree and through the shadow of the factory, toward the hills and woods at the edge of town.

"Poor soul," said Dorothy. "He used to be so lovely. And look at him now."

"**Kaboom!**" said Alec. "**Kapow!**" He flung the imaginary grenade. "Die, you traitor. Die!"

McTavish laughed. He straightened his tie and his black jacket.

"Well said, Bly," he said.

He waited as Alec and a bunch of other boys fell upon the pictures of German children and tore them to shreds.

He put the children into twos again and led them on toward the factory.

John picked up a scrap of paper that had escaped.

The boy on it had not completely gone. He seemed to be of John's own age.

 was written over him.

John folded it and put it into his pocket.

Walter Bloom was the gateman. He put a helmet on and limped out of his little gatehouse as McTavish led the children toward the factory through its shadows. He shook hands with McTavish. He had a black patch over one eye. He peered sternly through the other as he inspected the children.

"Any German spies among this lot, Mr. McTavish?" he said.

"You have your suspicions, Mr. Bloom?" said McTavish.

Bloom came to John, leaned toward him, stared at him.

"It is my duty," said Bloom, "to suspect everyone before I let them through these gates."

Alec giggled.

McTavish snarled a laugh.

"This boy, for instance," continued Bloom, leaning even closer. "He might look nice as ninepence, but . . ."

"Indeed," snorted McTavish. "I have often thought that that very one could be . . ."

"The enemy in our midst," said Bloom.

"Exactly," said McTavish.

"I am n-not!" John found himself saying.

Tears came to his eyes.

Bloom's face softened.

"Oh, son," he whispered. "Take no notice. I'm just kidding you."

His one eye closed quickly, like he was winking.

But he raised his voice again so that

McTavish could hear.

"Aye, nice as ninepence. But what dark secrets might be hidden in the heart?"

McTavish wiped the tears of laughter from his eyes.

"Indeed, Mr. Bloom!" he said.

"I am not . . ." said John again.

"Silence, boy!" McTavish roared. "And stop your sniveling!"

Bloom winked and smiled again.

"A bit of fun, that's all," he said.

He turned away and dragged open the massive metal gates.

He stood to attention as the children filed through.

John trembled. He thought of Jan in his pocket.

He found Dorothy at his side. She said to take no notice of cruel men like McTavish, of teasing men like Bloom.

"Remain within your twos!" snapped McTavish. "Do not speak unless you are spoken to! Touch nothing unless you are invited to!"

They went deeper into the factory.

They entered the din of machines and engines. Rattles and thuds, the scream of metal against metal, the thump of hammers, squeal of drills, clatter of chains, hisses and howls of escaping steam. It was as if a great war was being played out here, by the river, in this town, below that high blackened echoing metal roof.

And McTavish led them farther, and he paused and spread his arms wide open at the vision that lay before them.

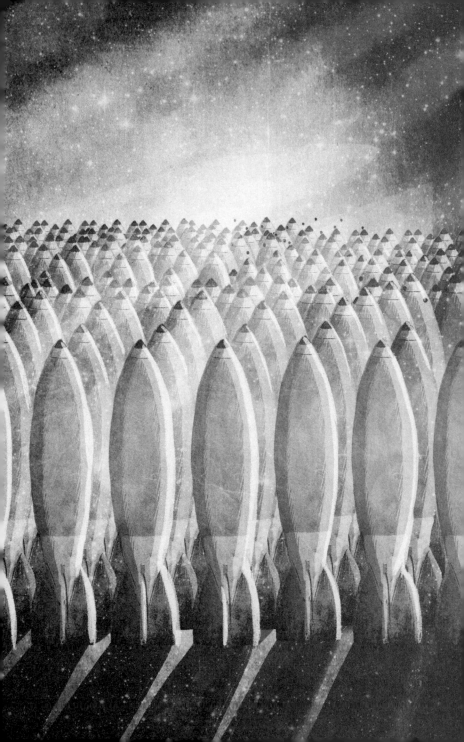

"We cannot go farther," he said. "We cannot go deeper into the factory's dangerous heart. But stand here with me, children. Feast your eyes on the wonders that are wrought here in this place!"

There were ranks of guns and gun carriages. There were cannons with their barrels tilted up like yearning arms. And there were shells, shells stacked high as houses. Shells no bigger than a fist and shells as big as babies, shells as big as boys, massive shells as big as men. There were dozens of them, hundreds, thousands. They gleamed in the light that poured from the garish bulbs above. John couldn't help himself. He reached out to touch. He pressed his warm, young hand to cold, hard metal. He thought of the shrapnel packed inside.

He thought of the explosions, of the shrapnel ripping its way through skin and bone and flesh. He thought of his dad in the trench, wearing the useless thin steel helmet.

"What were you told?" yelled McTavish. "Do not touch!"

John drew his hand away.

He looked beyond the wall of shells toward the factory's heart. That's where the machines were, where the gunpowder and shrapnel were, where the blue-dressed mothers created the weapons that would make the fathers safe. John searched for his mam with his eyes. He wanted to wave and for her to wave back. He wanted to find her and to run to her, but he could not discern her. The women seemed tiny, indistinguishable in their blue uniforms, were diminished by the vastness of the machines at which they worked. But then suddenly the women knew that the children were there, and some of them laughed to see them in this place. And they spread their arms and waved, and John was certain that one of them was his mam, and he waved and had to hold himself back from breaking free and running to her.

And then before them was a soldier, a soldier on crutches with a trouser leg pinned back to show his wooden leg. Some kind of officer in a helmet, with metal epaulets on his shoulders and a dead straight row of medals on his chest.

Despite the din, he didn't seem to need to raise his voice.

"Welcome, children," he announced. "I am

Major Hughes. As you see, I have been with the heroes. I have been with your brothers and fathers. And in this place, I am with heroes, too."

His voice was not like those of the children. It was what McTavish's voice, when he prayed, when he talked of the war, often seemed to want to be.

"Here," he said, "in this factory, is where the Great War will be won."

"When will it be won?" yelled someone, another boy yearning for his dad to be home again.

"When every rotten German's dead," laughed Alec.

Hughes shrugged.

"It could go on forever, children," he said.

Forever. The word thudded in John's heart.

"I do not think it will," continued Hughes. "But we are prepared to fight forever. We have the industry. We have the manpower. We have the *woman*power. And if it does go, just think on. You lads could be following your fathers. You lasses could be the women to keep the fathers safe."

He peered at the children.

"What do you think of that, children?"

"Let me at them!" Alec shouted.

"Yes!" said other boys. "Yes!"

John hung his head. Other children hung their heads.

Forever? wondered John again. *Forever and forever.*

"Good lads," said Hughes. "That's what we

old soldiers like to hear. That is what your *king* likes to hear. But it may not come to that. There are rumors that the enemy is on the run. There are rumors that it might all soon come to an end."

What rumors? John wanted to yell. *When will the war be done?*

"But we cannot relax," said the major. "Indeed, such rumors must lead us into ever greater effort." He gazed in wonder at the weapons that surrounded them. "This very afternoon," he said, "these products of our great industry will be loaded onto ships and carried down toward the battlefields. This is what the enemy understands. More guns, more bombs, more shells, more shells, and even more. These are the things that will bring him to his knees,

that will bring this war to an end. Pray for that day, children! Be good children! Fight along with us in your heart and in your soul."

John could not help himself.

He reached again, touched again. He gasped at the coldness of it, the hardness of it, the weight of it. He thought of the shrapnel packed inside, he thought of it exploding out, ripping through the skin and bone and flesh of Jan's father. He thought of his own flesh, so tender. He thought of all flesh, English, German, the tender flesh of all who lived and all who had ever lived.

When will it be over? he yelled inside himself.

"What were you told, you idiot?" howled McTavish.

John kept on, pressing his skin against the hard, cold metal.

"Imbecile!" yelled McTavish.

John felt McTavish's fist against his back.

And then

he

fell

and   knew

no more.

They carried him out on a stretcher.

He came to

as they laid him on the ground

outside the gates.

There was a nurse and Bloom the gateman, no one else. The others had continued with their factory tour.

Bloom peered down at him with his single eye.

"You OK, son?" he said.

John nodded.

For a moment, there was a tear in Bloom's eye.

"What we doing," he said softly, "bringing bairns like you to a place like this?"

He looked like he wanted to say more, but he just reached down and gently stroked John's forehead. Then he hissed a curse and limped back to his little gatehouse.

The nurse checked John's pulse, touched his brow and cheek, stared deep into his eyes.

"You'll be OK," she said. She smiled. "You're not the first one, son. And you'll not be the last."

She knelt beside him as he came properly back to his senses.

"Oh, look. This must be your mam coming out."

And then his mam was there, bending down to kiss and comfort him. There were pigeons in a tight flock flying over her, then the deep blue sky, the yellow sun.

"It's just a bit too much for some of them," the nurse said.

"Yes," murmured John's mam. "We all take it all for granted."

John struggled to sit up.

"I'm fine, Mam," he said. "Don't worry, Mam."

He touched her cheek. There were tiny scars, as always, caused by fragments of flying metal from the machines.

"You're such a brave boy, John," she said.

She looked back toward the factory.

"I can't stay," she said. "I have to go."

"I'm champion, Mam. Don't worry, Mam. See you when your shift's done, Mam."

"Are you sure?"

"Aye, course I am. I'm hard as nails, Mam."

She grinned and kissed him and wiped her eyes as she went back inside.

The nurse stayed with him some moments. She made him drink some water, she said she'd pray for him as she did for every child, and then she too went inside.

John stood up and walked away, out of the factory's shadow, back along the track of the river toward home. Inside, he sat at the little kitchen table and looked at Jan, the German boy from Düsseldorf. He ate a slice of bread with rose-hip jam.

He got some notepaper and wrote:

Dear Jan

I am a boy like you. I am
not at war with you. You are
not at war with me.

Your friend

John

He drew a picture of himself. He drew another of himself with his dad and mam, walking in the woods above the town. He put the letter and these pictures into an envelope. He addressed it to:

Jan
The German Boy
Düsseldorf
GERMANY

He put the picture of Jan back into his pocket and walked out again, to the square with the apple tree. A bunch of little children were dancing around the tree while an old man played a tin whistle. A newspaper billboard said:

John put the letter into the postbox there.

He walked through the narrow streets toward the woods beyond the edge of the town. The din of the munitions factory surrounded him.

The memory of the guns and shells came to him. A flock of pigeons turned to shells flying over the battlefield, then turned to birds again.

He shook the image from his head and kept on walking. He turned and looked back at the great factory building. Ships were being loaded on the jetties. One huge loaded ship was headed out toward the sea. He thought of his flimsy letter, heading out to Germany.

He walked on, away from the streets, and came to the grassy place where the town's children played their war games. They had dug trenches here. There were piles of stones that could be turned into grenades and shells. There were the dark scars of many fires. There were the scattered bones of rabbits that had been killed and cooked. There were trees where they tied up prisoners. The ground was battered and worn because the games had gone on for so long.

The air continued to echo with the factory's endless din. It turned to the din of war for John. He slipped into some kind of dream, and the place of children's games became the battlefields of France. He heard the explosions and the screams. The ground shuddered. There were foxholes and potholes and barbed wire. John saw the dead and dying. He smelled gunpowder and smoke and the stench of burning flesh. He heard the screams. He saw men running with their rifles and bayonets held out before them.

He tried to discern his dad, but in their uniforms all men looked the same. All were diminished by the vastness of the battle they were in. He tried to look across the battlefield, trying to discern a soldier who might be the father of Jan, but could see nothing that made sense. He fell again and must have lost consciousness again, and when he woke the place became the place of children's games again.

The sun had fallen in the sky. The leaves of the wood were blazing yellow, golden, brown and red, but just a few steps in they were dark and shadowy. He went to the edge of the wood, where the briar roses flourished. He felt the hips, seeking the softest, ripest ones. He bit the tips and squeezed them and licked the soft sweet flesh that seeped out there, then stripped the skin away. The inner skin was an irritant. He knew his fingers would be sore tonight. But he kept on opening, lifting the seeds out, harvesting them. He threw handfuls of them across the earth, all those little ones, all those tiny seeds of life, and let them scatter where they would. He went on gathering, casting. He imagined a field of wild briar roses growing where the war games were once played. He imagined the hips that would be harvested, the jars of jam that would be created and eaten by generations of children still to come.

There were children coming. He heard voices and running feet. And here was Alec and some other boys come to play again.

Alec's eyes were all aglitter with the excitements of the munitions factory.

He laughed at John.

"Couldn't take it, eh?" he called. "Namby-pamby, eh?"

He lifted a rock and flung it into the shadowy woods. He flung another. He pointed into the dark and screamed with hatred and delight.

"There they are!" he yelled. "See them? The enemy!"

"Aye!" another called.

"Get them!" called another.

"Howay, lads! Let's get the blasted Hun!"

And off they went, and the woods were filled with their screaming, their yelled explosions, their *ratatatats*, their cries of terror, pain and death. Their noise faded as they went farther in.

"Good riddance," said someone at John's back.

Dorothy.

And there were others. Someone lit a fire and rolled potatoes into it.

"I hope," said Dorothy, "they don't come across Uncle Gordon."

They all murmured their assent.

"I wish," said Dorothy, "that it would all just come to an end."

"Amen," said someone.

The flames glowed brightly in the quickly fading light.

They sat on stones there and ate blackened half-cooked spuds.

In the darkness, one or two children wept.

Far off, in the woods, the screams of the warriors faded as they went deeper in.

After a time, a shadowy figure came out from the woods and shuffled toward them.

"Uncle Gordon!" whispered Dorothy.

They didn't speak but welcomed him into their circle. He sat beside his niece. She asked if he was all right and he answered yes.

"As far as anybody can be all right these days," he said.

Then he laughed gently.

"Silly lads," he said. "They ran right past me and didn't see a thing. Fine soldiers they'd make, eh?"

John handed him a hot potato, and he ate and said it was delicious.

He looked at all the faces, glowing in the firelight. He held up a white feather, so brilliant in the dark.

"They say it's a thing of shame," he said. "But the truth is that I'm proud of it."

He held it out on the flat of his hand, and John took it from him. He inspected its lightness, its delicacy, its beauty.

"Keep it," said Gordon. "If you'd like to."

"I will," said John.

The others caught their breath.

"Keep it hid," said someone.

John tucked it inside his shirt.

Deep in the woods, an owl was hooting.

Gordon left them, heading back toward his hiding places.

John watched him leave and saw him pass another figure at the farthest edge of the firelight.

John saw that it was Jan, the German boy from Düsseldorf, standing where the rose hips grew.

John said that he was going for a pee. He left the others and went toward his friend.

"Hello," he said softly.

"Guten Abend," said Jan.

The two boys were the same height, the same age.

They gazed at each other for an impossible moment.

There was nothing they could do. They were children in the dark. They were children, yearning for safety, yearning for love, yearning for the war to end.

"I am not at war!" said John at last.

"Ich bin nicht im Krieg!" said Jan.

They moved closer toward each other.

Then here came the stupid noise of Alec and his avenging warriors again, and Jan was gone.

The factory glared as John headed home again. It thundered and dinned below the endless stars. Lit ships moved downriver toward the pitch-black sea. He walked across the apple-tree square and entered the flow of women streaming home from the factory at shift's end. Some of them touched him tenderly, some of them murmured his name. Some were singing and there was much bright laughter. He looked for his mam, but he couldn't see her yet.

He got home just before her. The door was open. The two policemen from that morning were sitting at the table. They had his drawings, his letter, his envelope. They held them up to show him.

"What is *this*?" said one.

"Do you know," said the other, "what treason is, and what we do to traitors?"

John's heart seemed to stop. He couldn't speak.

"Do you *know*?"

"Y-yes."

"Yes! And do you want to feel that noose around your neck?"

They tore the papers into tiny pieces before his eyes. They scattered them onto the floor.

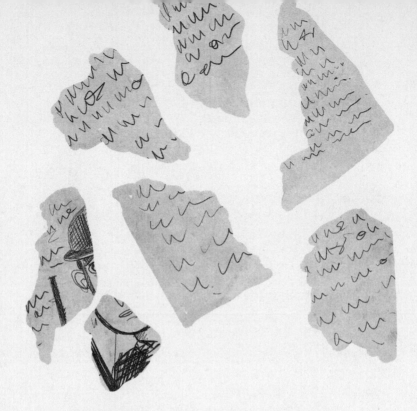

"Who else you been writing to?" they

snapped.

"N-nobody."

"Nobody?"

"The k-king."

One turned his face away. He put his arm

across his face to cover his snorted laughter.

"The k-king?" said the other. "Who else?"

"The Archbishop of C-c . . ."

They burst out laughing. They tried to keep their faces straight. They calmed themselves and became stern again.

"And what did the *k-king* and the archbishop say to you?"

"N-nothing."

"Sensible king. Clever archbishop. Better things to do than correspond with traitors. What else you done, boy?"

"N-n . . ."

"What *else*?"

"Mebbe we should search the place."

"Mebbe we should search *him*."

John felt the feather, tender against the skin of his chest.

He stopped himself from reaching down toward the picture of Jan in his pocket.

"Mebbe we should get him behind bars."

Then the door opened again and his mam was here.

"What's going on?" she said.

She rushed to John and held him.

"You brung up a traitor, missus," said the tall one.

"*What?*"

"Aye. Could be a trip to the gallows for him."

"*What?*"

"He'll explain."

And they were gone.

John held out the picture to her.

She gently touched Jan's face with her finger.

"Jan from Düsseldorf," she read. "A German boy. Can that be true?"

"Yes. Dorothy's uncle Gordon had it."

"*Him?*"

"Yes. He's been to Germany. He's seen German children."

"But he's . . ."

"He's what, Mam? So I wrote a letter to Jan. And the policemen found it and that's it on the floor."

She picked up the pieces and tried to put them in order.

"Am I a traitor, Mam?" he said.

"No."

"That's what they said. I told Jan he was my friend. I told him I wasn't at war with him. Look, you can read it there. Am I a traitor?"

"Oh, son."

"I'm *not* at war with him, Mam, am I?"

She didn't answer. She looked away. He wanted to tell her about seeing Jan by the woods, but he couldn't.

"Look at him," he said. "He's just like me."

"Just like *you*?"

"Yes. Look at him, Mam."

She was crying now.

"I'm sure he's a lovely boy," she whispered, but he didn't believe that she believed it.

"I'm sure his dad loves him," she said, "and I'm sure his mam loves him, too."

"Are you, Mam?"

"Yes."

She put her arms around him and she held him close and she felt the feather.

He took it from inside his shirt, and she recoiled.

"What's that?" she gasped. "Put it away. Get rid of it!"

He held it in his hand.

"It came from Dorothy's uncle, too," he said.

"Him again?" she gasped.

"Yes. What's wrong with him? Why does everybody hate him so?"

"Because," she whispered.

"Because why? Because he doesn't want to fight?"

"I don't know, John. It's too much for me to think about, John. Throw the feather away, John."

"No! Look at it. It's beautiful."

"*Beautiful?*"

"Do you think I'm a coward, Mam?" he said.

"*What?* A coward?
My boy, a coward?"

"You do, don't you?"

"No. No!"

Both of them were
crying now. He held the
feather tight.

"Why do you do
it, Mam?" he sobbed
at last.

"Do what?"

"Make shrapnel
shells? Why do
you make shrapnel
shells?"

She just cried, and
wouldn't answer.

"You told me what they do," he said. "Why do you make them?"

"It's my work. It's what I do."

"But *why*?"

"Because we are at war."

"But why? Why?"

"Stop it, John. Some things are not for us to know."

"What things, Mam?"

"Stop it, I said! And throw those stupid things away!"

And she stood up and retreated from him.

That night he said his prayers as always. He clutched the white feather to his chest. He kept the picture of Jan beneath his pillow. In his dreams he went to Germany, to Düsseldorf. It was just like here. A town and a river and some woods and lots of children playing. There were German voices and English voices all mixed up. There were pigeons in the sky that stayed as pigeons.

Uncle Gordon was there. He had a nest in his hair, and there were cheeping chicks in the nest. John's mam and dad danced in each other's arms around a huge blossoming apple tree. Alec Bly and his friends were doing acrobatics, climbing onto one another's shoulders and making a pyramid, like they were in a circus. They laughed when they tumbled and started to climb on one another again. The two policemen had grown very fat, and they lay close together snoring in the sun while bright-winged butterflies gathered on their dark uniforms. Mr. McTavish concentrated hard, trying to play the violin. The king and the archbishop strolled arm in arm, admiring each other's robes. It looked like there had once been a factory by the river, but now it had fallen down. Moss and turf and wildflowers had grown over it, and briar roses flourished at its edge.

The air was warm.

Birds sang.

The sun shone down.

He dreamed this dream each night as time went on.

One morning, as he ate his breakfast of jam and bread and tea, he nervously started to tell his mam about it. She was fastening the buttons of her blue uniform. He'd heard her crying in the night. He could see that her eyes were still glazed with tears.

"Mam," he started, "I get this dream."

She turned her head away and let him go no further.

"Dreams?" she snapped. She glared at him. "What good are dreams at times like this?"

He ran out the door, heading for school.

He'd gone a hundred yards or so before he heard her running behind him. She caught his shoulder and pulled him to her.

"Oh, son," she sobbed. "I'm so sorry, son."

And they hugged each other in the street while the factory workers and the school children streamed past.

Only the stupid ones, like Alec Bly, laughed at this.

After that, she listened when he told her. Once, she admitted that she wasn't really listening.

"It's just your voice I want to hear," she said. "I can hear the love in it. It's like listening to a song or a prayer. It calms me so."

He put his arms around her, as if he was looking after her, as if he was the adult and she was a tiny child.

Autumn deepened, darkened, and the dreams went on.

Each night in his sleep, he encountered Jan. They couldn't talk together much, but they showed each other by their eyes and their gestures that they were friends. They ate potatoes together and wrote stories and drew pictures together. They played football and dozens of German and English kids joined in. John showed Jan who his parents were, and Jan said they looked *schön*. Jan showed another young man and woman, and John understood that these were his friend's parents. He whispered that they were beautiful.

"Do you think," John asked his mam one morning, "if I dream hard enough, that the dream might come true?"

"That a dream could bring about the end of the war?" she said.

"Yes, Mam."

"Who knows? Maybe a dream's as good as anything."

"As good as prayers?"

"Oh, John, I don't dare say that. How can anything be as good as prayers?"

"As good as shrapnel shells, then?"

His mam touched the tiny wounds on her cheek.

"Aye, John, maybe they're as good as shrapnel shells. Much better than those damn shrapnel shells."

Outside the dream, the war went on. John's dad fought in France with a thousand other dads. His mam went to the factory with a thousand other mams. Ship after ship carried weapons down to France. John went to school. He did his work. He said his prayers.

He tried and failed to recall his father's face.

The days dragged. They grew darker and colder and were tinged with endless fear. John wanted every day to end. He wanted to enter his sleep, to be carried into his dream. It seemed that the world would always be like this, that it had always been like this, that war would be forever and forever.

When the end came, it happened very fast.

John heard the voice ringing through his dreams. He heard it ringing through the street. He opened his eyes and rubbed them. Sunlight was peeping through the curtains. He wasn't sure if he was awake. Maybe this was some new aspect of the dream.

The indecipherable voice went on. There were other voices joining in: laughter, cheers, howls and screams.

He got up, looked out.

Mr. Bloom, the gatekeeper, was out there. He was running past the houses with his arms held high.

"It's over!" he yelled and yelled again. "The war is over!"

People were peeping like John from their

bedroom windows, were beginning to stream from their doors.

Bloom looked up and saw John's face. He stopped. He yelled, "It's true, son! It's true!"

And people began to hold up newspapers and newspaper billboards with the news.

GERMANY SURRENDERS. GREAT WAR TO END. PEACE! PEACE!

The words were repeated and called and sung all along the street. Factory sirens began to blare, church bells to ring. And John's mam was at his side and holding him tight, and he leaned back into her. She gasped his name, and the words rose from her body and broke from her mouth as if they'd been confined inside her for a thousand years.

"Oh, John. The war is over."

One day in mid-December, icy deep midwinter, John came home from school to find a man in uniform sitting at the kitchen table. He didn't know him. The man didn't seem to know him. John's mam held the man's hand.

"This is your daddy, John," she said.

"My dad?"

The man raised his hand and started to chew his fingers. There was a long scar on his cheek. He took his fingers from his mouth and licked his lips.

"Hello, son," he said.

John didn't know what to say, didn't know what to do. He just stood there in the doorway where he'd stopped. For a moment he wanted to step out again into the dusk.

"I came back," said the man. His voice was trembling. "We had to stay on in France for a while to sort things out."

He reached down to a brown paper parcel on the floor.

"Look," he said, lifting some clothes out. "They gave me a suit to wear."

He hung his head. Tears dripped to the table.

"Give us a hug, son, eh?" he whispered.

And John stepped forward, and that's what he did, and what all of them did, as they hugged one another tight and the sun sank fast outside.

A week later on an icy, sunny Sunday afternoon, after everyone had been to church and prayed and given thanks to the Lord, the whole town gathered in the square around the apple tree.

There were tables loaded with pies and cakes. There was beer and tea. A brass band played. Children played and adults danced. There were limping men and limbless men and bandaged men, and there were missing men.

John's dad and mam danced. Sometimes they held each other very tight, sometimes very tenderly. They kept turning their eyes and their smiles to their son.

He kept smiling back at them. He had begun to feel happy — maybe as happy as he had been when he was very small, before there was any war at all, but he couldn't be certain, because he couldn't really remember that time or remember that boy.

He stood with Dorothy and some of her friends. She said she'd gone into the woods with cakes for her Uncle Gordon, and she'd asked him to come out, but he'd said he felt he'd have to hide forever now.

The sun reddened as it fell toward the woods, and the people in the square were reddened, too. John found himself wondering if he was asleep in bed, if this day was a dream, if peace was a dream. He wondered if all life and everything in it was nothing but a dream. Beyond the square, the roof of the factory was dead straight and black against the sky. Its gates were locked now. The women had left their work. John wondered what would happen to the factory now. What would happen to the shells that were still stacked high inside it that had not been shipped to France? What would the machines and engines be used for now? What would the ships carry downriver toward the sea?

When the band paused between tunes, there came a low, deep groaning from the factory, a kind of snoring, as if the factory itself was asleep.

John turned his mind from this and turned it to his dream of Jan. He knew what he must do, now that he was getting older.

When he has left school, when he is a man, he will go to Germany. He will find his friend Jan, the German boy from Düsseldorf. If he doesn't find that Jan, he will find other Jans and be friends with them. They will all see that people from England and Germany are just the same.

He will take gifts for them, rose hips
crammed with tiny seeds, and they'll open
them together

and scatter those seeds across the German earth,

and they'll watch them grow.